Andy Shane

and the
Queen of Egypt

Jennifer Richard Jacobson

illustrated by Abby Carter

CANDLEWICK PRESS

For my Uncle Bob — Let me entertain you
J. R. J.

To Carter and Samantha
A. C.

Text copyright © 2008 by Jennifer Richard Jacobson
Illustrations copyright © 2008 by Abby Carter

First paperback edition 2009

The Library of Congress has cataloged the hardcover edition as follows:

Jacobson, Jennifer, date.
Andy Shane and the Queen of Egypt / Jennifer Jacobson ; illustrated by Abby Carter.
—1st ed.
p.   cm.
Summary: Andy Shane selects Egypt as the topic of his first-ever Culture Fair project,
but the very bossy Dolores Starbuckle declares that she is the Queen of Egypt
and does not give him a moment's peace until he agrees to let her work with him.
ISBN 978-0-7636-3211-3 (hardcover)
[1. Cooperativeness—Fiction. 2. Schools—Fiction. 3. Bossiness—Fiction.
4. Behavior—Fiction.]   I. Carter, Abby, ill. II. Title.
PZ7.J1529Amd 2008
[E]—dc22   2007032003

ISBN 978-0-7636-4404-8 (paperback)

2 4 6 8 10 9 7 5 3 1

Printed in the United States of America

This book was typeset in Vendome.
The illustrations were done in black pencil and black watercolor wash.

Candlewick Press
99 Dover Street
Somerville, Massachusetts 02144

visit us at www.candlewick.com

CONTENTS

1

I Am the Queen

Andy Shane parked his bike and
shifted the weight in his backpack.
"Let's meet by the *tree* when the
clock says *three*," he said.

"I will ride my *bike,* or we will have to *hike,*" said Granny Webb.

Granny and Andy had been talking in rhymes all morning. It was hard to stop once you got started.

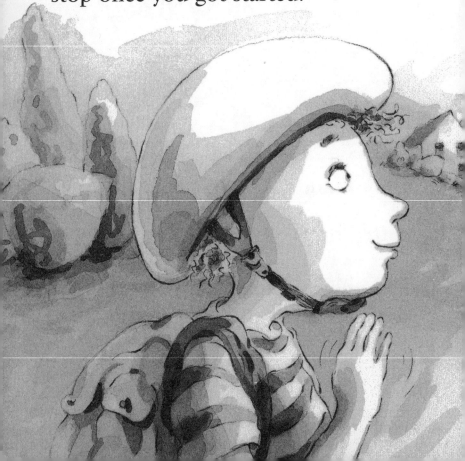

"Oh, wait!" said Granny.

"Don't be *late,*" said Andy, waving good-bye.

"No, really," called Granny Webb.

"I have something for you."

Andy turned back to see what
Granny was pulling from her pocket.
Whatever it was appeared to be on
the end of a long gold chain.

"Oooh," said Andy, moving
closer. It was a dark green bug
frozen in clear plastic. "A beetle!"

"A scarab beetle!" said Granny.

"Is this Egyptian?" asked Andy.

Andy knew that the scarab beetle was important to the people of ancient Egypt.

"I think so," said Granny Webb, handing it to Andy. "I knew you were thinking about African countries last night, and a memory of it popped into my *head* while I was heading off to *bed*!"

Andy laughed at Granny's rhyme. "Thanks," he said, and *he* headed into school.

"What do you think of my new sandals, Andy Shane?" asked Dolores Starbuckle as they sat down at their desks.

"Cool," said Andy.

"I made them myself with milk cartons and glitter," said Dolores.

Andy noticed that Dolores Starbuckle was particularly fancy this morning.

"I hope each of you has chosen an African country," said Ms. Janice. "We need to get ready for the school Culture Fair."

Dolores Starbuckle sat up as tall as she could.

"Polly," said Ms. Janice with her pen in the air, ready to write, "what country would you like to learn about?"

"Kenya," said Polly. "My uncle went to Kenya."

Kenya was a large country with deserts and rain forests. Andy had *almost* chosen Kenya.

"Ahmed?" asked Ms. Janice.

"The Gambia."

Ms. Janice told the class that The Gambia was a small farming country. Andy thought he might like to be a farmer one day.

"Andy Shane?"

Andy touched his pocket. "Egypt," he said softly.

"I'm sorry, Andy," said Ms. Janice. "I didn't hear you."

"I think he said Ethiopia," said Dolores. She was always trying to be helpful.

"Is that right, Andy?" asked Ms. Janice.

Andy shook his head.

"Do you mean Nigeria, Andy Shane?" said Dolores. "I think you mean Ni-*geeeeee*-ria."

"Egypt," Andy said more loudly.

"But you can't choose Egypt," said

Dolores, springing out of her seat.

"I'm wearing my white Egyptian

clothes and my gold jewelry. I even

made sandals. I am the QUEEN

of Egypt."

The class laughed.

Andy slumped down on his desk.

Why did Dolores Starbuckle always

insist on getting what *she* wanted?

But he couldn't argue with her—

not in front of the whole class!

Andy knew everyone was waiting for his answer. He wished he could disappear altogether.

"We'll work this out later," said Ms. Janice. She finished calling on the children. Then she told the class to line up for a visit to the library, where they could begin their research. "Andy Shane," she said, "you're line leader."

Dolores stood in front of Andy.

"Andy Shane, you know I *loooove*
Egypt!" she said. "I even have a
model of a sphinx!"

"What's a sphinx?" asked Polly.

"A statue. Mine has a lion's body
with a bird's head," said Dolores.

"Weird," said Polly.

"But I have this," said Andy.

He pulled out the beetle.

"Oooh," said Dolores, admiring
the necklace. She sighed a long, deep
sigh. Then her face brightened. "Can
we work together, Andy Shane?"

Andy didn't know what to say. He liked to take his time with ideas, see how they felt. And right now, he did not feel like giving Dolores her way. "I'll think about it," he said.

2

Pineapple Pyramids

That night, like every Tuesday night when her father and mother went to choir practice, Dolores ate dinner with Andy Shane and Granny Webb.

Andy was on the kitchen floor coloring a picture of a sphinx when Dolores arrived.

"I wish I could draw like you," said Dolores.

Andy looked up to say thanks, but Dolores was already busy tying on her favorite Granny Webb apron—the one with the big pockets. She hopped up on the stool near the counter.

Granny Webb was emptying chunks of pineapple from a can into a bowl.

"I'll do that, Granny Webb," said

Dolores. "I like to be helpful."

Granny Webb smiled and handed

Dolores the can.

"Wow!" said Dolores. "I never noticed that before."

Andy wanted to say, "Noticed what?" But Dolores went right on talking.

"May I serve the pineapple pizza tonight? *Please?*" asked Dolores.

"Well, it's Andy's turn to set the table, but I'm sure he wouldn't mind some help. Isn't that right, Andy?"

"Sure," said Andy.

After Granny took the pizza from the oven and let it cool, Dolores carefully arranged slices on each plate. Then she stood back and admired her work.

"My, my, my," said Granny Webb.

Andy came over to see what the fuss was about. "What *is* this?" he asked.

"Why, Andy," said Granny, "it's pineapple pizza. One of your favorites."

"But how come the pineapple is all piled up on the side of the plate?" asked Andy.

"Don't you see?" said Dolores. "The pineapple chunks are little bricks. I made you a pineapple pyramid!"

"But how come the pizza has bald spots?" said Andy, pointing to his plate. "The pizza and the pineapple are supposed to be together!"

"Think about it, Andy Shane," said Dolores. "The most popular booths at the Culture Fair always have food samples. If we work together on the project, I can make lots and lots of pineapple pyramids! We'll be a huge hit!"

"Oh, brother," said Andy.

Andy knew that Dolores was looking at him while he ate, hoping he'd cave in and say they could work together. But the only thing that caved in that night was his pineapple pyramid.

3

Walk Like an Egyptian

When Andy walked into his classroom the next day, he noticed two things. Number one, Ms. Janice's big yellow bag with orange flowers on it was not beside her desk.

And number two, in the center of Ms. Janice's desk was a giant stack of paper. This could mean only one thing.

Andy Shane looked at Dolores.

Dolores Starbuckle nodded.

They were having a substitute teacher.

Sure enough, a tall man came into the room, explained that Ms. Janice was not feeling well, and handed out work sheets.

Andy finished all the math problems on the page. Then he began drawing pictures of baseballs and baseball bats all around the edge of his paper. According to Andy Shane, today was the best day of the year. It was the first day of T-ball!

Dolores cleared her throat.

Andy looked up to see what she was doing.

She was writing their names in Egyptian hieroglyphs.

Andy pretended he didn't see.

The tall man handed out a second set of work sheets, and then a third. When Dolores had finished her third paper, she asked the substitute teacher if they could make get-well cards for Ms. Janice.

"A wonderful suggestion!" said the substitute.

Andy Shane reached into his desk to find his crayons. He pulled out his action figure of Giraffe Man.

"Hey!" he cried. His Giraffe Man was wrapped up in toilet paper.

"Doesn't he make a great mummy?" asked Dolores.

"Ugh!" said Andy. After he finished his card, he would draw a sign for his desk that read *No Trespassing.*

That evening, Andy's coach asked Andy to play right field. In T-ball, you have to have a strong arm to play right field.

Andy Shane looked at the bleachers to locate Granny Webb. Sitting next to Granny was Dolores Starbuckle. Andy Shane couldn't help noticing that she was *still* wearing her fancy Egyptian clothes.

Both teams had batters that had no trouble hitting the ball off the tee. By the final inning, the score was tied. A girl known as Slugger was up next. Andy adjusted his cap and backed up. He would be ready.

Suddenly, music blared from the stands. Dolores was standing on the top bleacher. Only she wasn't just standing. She was dancing. She was dancing to a song called "Walk Like an Egyptian."

Andy knew that Dolores loved this song. She loved showing others how she could walk like an Egyptian along with the music. She strutted and turned, strutted and turned.

People in the stands applauded.

But Slugger wasn't watching Dolores. She got into position, pulled back the bat, and popped that ball into right field.

"Catch it, Andy!" yelled Granny Webb.

But Andy didn't catch it. He was too busy watching Dolores. So were the other kids in the outfield.

The ball rolled past Andy and hit

the back fence.

Slugger scored a home run, and her team won the game.

Andy Shane would not even look at Dolores when he came off the field.

At that moment, she was not the queen of anything.

4
A Team

That night Andy couldn't get to sleep.

First, he couldn't believe he had

missed the ball and lost the game.

Second, he knew that tomorrow he had to stand up and tell the class his plans for the Culture Fair. Whenever Andy had to speak to the whole class, he felt as if his throat took a dive and hid somewhere deep in his stomach.

"Here's a 'sorry' note," said Dolores as Andy walked through the classroom door. It was in Egyptian hieroglyphs.

"Do you want me to read it to you?" asked Dolores.

"No," Andy said. He didn't even try to read it. He just stuffed it into his pocket.

Later, when the class was painting an enormous map of the continent of Africa, Dolores handed Andy the paintbrush with the blue handle. Everyone in Ms. Janice's class knew that the brush with the blue handle was the biggest and the best of all.

"No, thanks," said Andy. He didn't even look at Dolores when he spoke.

When the painting was finished, Ms. Janice asked each student to come to the front of the room and give a report on his or her Culture Day plans.

Peter went first. He showed the class pictures of masks from Mali. "I'm going to make a mask," he said.

Polly showed the class a mobile
she was working on. Hanging from
the mobile were pictures of the desert,
the forest, the seashore, and a big
city. All of these places were in
Kenya.

"Andy, show us what you've done," said Ms. Janice.

Andy walked to the front of the room. He began to speak but realized he had nothing in his hands. Peter had shown something. Polly had shown something. What should he do?

"I want—" Andy paused. "I want . . ."

"Your mummy!" said Dolores.

Everyone laughed.

Dolores reached into Andy's desk and took out Giraffe Man. She handed him to Andy.

"Oooh," the students said.

Andy Shane held the mummy action figure but still looked as if he didn't know what to say.

Dolores waved her hands from the

back of the room to get

his attention.

She made

her hands go

around her neck,

like a necklace.

"I have a necklace," said Andy, "that

has a scarab beetle on it. People in

ancient Egypt believed that the

scarab-beetle god pushed the sun

across the sky. And . . ."

"Yes, Andy?" said Ms. Janice.

Dolores made her hands and face look like the sphinx that Andy had drawn at home.

"Oh, I made a picture of a sphinx," said Andy.

"You should see Andy's picture, Ms. Janice," said Dolores. "It came out really well!"

Andy could feel his face getting warmer, but he was happy. He took a big breath and sat down.

"Thank you, Andy," said Ms. Janice. "Dolores, why don't you come up and tell us about the country you've chosen."

Dolores walked to the front of the room.

She pointed to the map the children had painted and said, "I've chosen the teeny tiny country of Togo, which is—"

"No!" shouted Andy.

All eyes turned to him.

"Andy?" said Ms. Janice.

Andy stood up. "Dolores and I are going to work together—on Egypt."

"Really?" asked Dolores.

Andy nodded.

"Oh, thank you, thank you, thank you, Andy Shane!"

For a minute, Andy was afraid Dolores was going to hug him. Or she was going to strut back and forth doing her Egyptian dance. Instead,

she simply wiggled her toes in her

Egyptian sandals and smiled.

"Wonderful," said Ms. Janice.

Andy smiled back. There was no doubt about it. He and Dolores Starbuckle, the Queen of Egypt, would make a great team.

Check out Andy and Dolores's adventures!

Jennifer Richard Jacobson
illustrated by Abby Carter

www.candlewick.com